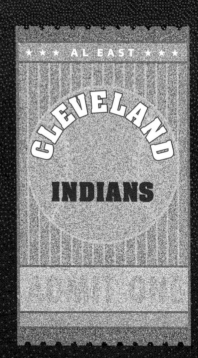

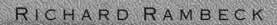

RICHARD RAMBECK

Published by Creative Education, Inc.

123 S. Broad Street, Mankato, Minnesota 56001

Art Director, Rita Marshall
Cover and title page design by Virginia Evans
Cover and title page illustration by Rob Day
Type set by FinalCopy Electronic Publishing
Book design by Rita Marshall

Photos by Allsport, Campion, UPI/Bettmann
and Wide World Photos

Library of Congress Cataloging-in-Publication Data

Rambeck, Richard.

   Cleveland Indians / by Richard Rambeck.

   p. cm.

   Summary: A history of Cleveland's baseball club,
whose home base of Municipal Stadium is the largest
facility used by a team in major league baseball.

   ISBN 0-88682-439-7

   1. Cleveland Indians (Baseball team)—History—
Juvenile literature. [1. Cleveland Indians (Baseball
team)—History. 2. Baseball—History.] I. Title.
GV875.C7R36 1991   91-10385
796.357'64'0977132—dc20   CIP

THE EARLY YEARS

Although Cleveland is not located in the middle of Ohio, it is certainly one of the major centers of the state's economy. Cleveland, Ohio's largest metropolis, with more than 535,000 people, is a busy port city in the northeastern corner of the state. Cleveland is located right on Lake Erie, one of the five Great Lakes. Ships that carry goods up and down the St. Lawrence Seaway dock on Cleveland's waterfront.

Lake Erie dominates the view from just about any location in the city, and is responsible for many of Cleveland's weather patterns, as heavy winds often blow inland off the lake. One of the structures most affected by the Lake Erie winds is Cleveland's Municipal Stadium, home of both the

Cy Young played in Cleveland from 1909 to 1911.

Cleveland Browns of the National Football League and the Cleveland Indians of professional baseball.

Municipal Stadium, which will soon be replaced by a new facility, is the largest in major-league baseball. Although the Cleveland baseball club rarely comes close to filling the giant stadium, the team has provided its fans with plenty of excitement over the past several decades. The Cleveland club, which was one of the charter members of the American League, had several names between 1901 and 1915. Unfortunately, the team had little success. But that started to change when the franchise became known as the Indians in 1916.

Led by star center fielder Tristan Speaker, the Indians began moving up in the American League standings. Speaker, who became the manager as well in 1919, and pitcher Steve Bagby gave the Cleveland fans cause to hope for an American League pennant. The Indians would win the pennant in 1920, but the team would also have to cope with a tragedy.

On August 20 the Indians were in New York for a first-place showdown with the Yankees. Cleveland shortstop Ray Chapman, who was Speaker's best friend, was hit on the head by a pitch from New York's Carl Mays. The blow fractured Chapman's skull, and about fifteen hours after the game, he died in a New York hospital, the only player ever killed as a result of an injury suffered in a major-league game. The grief-stricken Speaker and the rest of the Indians didn't want to continue playing, but they soon decided to dedicate the season—and their pennant hopes—to Chapman's memory. Cleveland went on to win its first American League pennant and earned the right to play the Brooklyn Dodgers in a best-of-nine-games World

1 9 0 1

In the inaugural season of the American League, Ollie Pickering led Cleveland with a .309 average.

Reliever Doug Jones has frequently excited Cleveland fans.

Series. Led by Bagby, who won the crucial fifth game with the series tied two games apiece, the Indians won the championship five games to two. It was a great moment in Cleveland sports history. Unfortunately, the Indians and their fans would have to wait almost thirty years for their next taste of glory.

1 9 3 3

Hal Trosky drove in 142 runs on his way to becoming the AL's Rookie of the Year.

CLEVELAND FINDS FELLER ON THE FARM

Cleveland and the rest of the American League took a backseat to the powerful New York Yankees throughout the 1920s. In the late 1920s and 1930s, both the Philadelphia Athletics and the Detroit Tigers also produced powerful teams. The Indians, however, remained one of the American League's also-rans. Then, in 1936, they found the player who would eventually pitch them back to the top.

"Gentlemen," said Cleveland team executive Cy Slapnicka at a private luncheon, "I've found the greatest young pitcher I ever saw. I suppose this sounds like the same old stuff to you, but I want you to believe me. This boy that I found out in Iowa will be the greatest pitcher the world has ever known. I only saw him pitch once before I signed him." The other team executives looked excitedly at Slapnicka. Who was this guy? they wanted to know. "Bob Feller," Slapnicka told them. "When can we see him?" they asked. "Bob's finishing out his school term," Slapnicka said, "but I repeat to you, gentlemen, he will be the star of them all. Do you know that he averaged ninteen strikeouts a game last summer?"

The executives were impressed, but many of them thought Feller was finishing out his college term. When

8

Slapnicka told them Feller was a seventeen-year-old high school student, many wondered if Slapnicka hadn't lost his mind. A week later they all found out about Feller, the polite, simple farm boy with a devastating fastball. He pitched three innings for the Indians in an exhibi tion game against the St. Louis Cardinals. Steve O'Neill, the Cleveland catcher who doubled as the manager, caught two of the innings and then came to the bench complaining of a sore hand. "That kid's too tough for me to catch," O'Neill said. "He throws that thing so fast it looks like a pea."

1 9 4 0

Bob Feller became the first pitcher in history to throw a no-hitter on opening day.

The Cardinals must have felt the same way, as Feller struck out eight of the nine St. Louis batters he faced. After the game a photographer asked Cardinal pitcher Dizzy Dean, a future Hall-of-Famer, if he'd pose with Feller. "Why ask me?" Dean laughed. "Ask the kid if he'll pose with me!"

A few weeks later, Feller struck out fifteen St. Louis Browns batters in his first regular-season game. In his next game, he matched Dizzy Dean's major-league strikeout record by fanning seventeen Philadelphia Athletics. Feller soon became the talk of the American League; he also became one of the top pitchers. By the time he was in his early twenties, Feller was consistently winning at least twenty games a season. But the United States had become involved in World War II, and young men were called to fight for their country. Feller enlisted in the Navy after winning twenty-five games in 1941.

Feller missed four full seasons while in the service. There is no telling how many more games Feller would have won and how many more players he would have struck out had he not lost those seasons. When he

Greg Swindell, another Cleveland ace.

Ex-Cleveland outfielder Cory Snyder.

The hustling Lou Boudreau (right) led the Indians to the AL pennant.

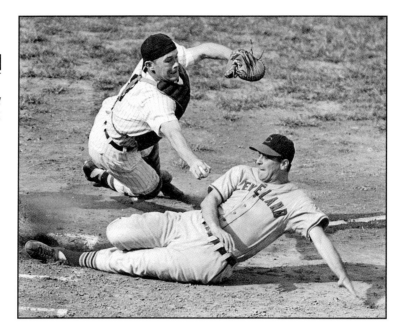

returned to baseball, though, he was as good as ever, winning twenty-six games in 1946. Thanks to Feller and shortstop Lou Boudreau, who was also the manager, the Indians had hopes of contending for a pennant.

In 1948 the Indians won their first six games and were still in first place on June 30, much to the amazement of the other teams in the league. "Don't worry about the Indians," said one American League manager. "They'll fall apart; they always do." But the Indians didn't fall apart; Lou Boudreau wouldn't let them. The Cleveland short-stop batted .355 and was named the American League's Most Valuable Player. The Indians also got outstanding performances from veteran pitchers Bob Lemon and the ageless Leroy "Satchel" Paige, a black man who finally made his major-league debut in his late forties.

Ultimately, the Indians and the Boston Red Sox tied

for first place in the American League, forcing a one-game playoff to decide who would win the pennant. Neither Feller nor Lemon was available to pitch the play-off game, but it really didn't matter who was on the mound because Boudreau destroyed the Red Sox with two home runs and two singles. Cleveland defeated Boston 8–3 to advance to the World Series against another team from Boston, the Braves.

In the World Series, Feller's effectiveness was reduced because of a sore arm. But Bob Lemon, who posted a 20–14 record during the regular season, was razor-sharp. Lemon won both his starts as the Indians defeated the Braves four games to two, giving Cleveland its second World Series title.

The Indians remained one of the top teams in the American League for several seasons, but they weren't able to win another pennant until 1954. That year Cleveland put together the most victories ever by an American League team in a season, winning 111 and losing only forty-three. The main reason for the team's success was outstanding pitching. Bob Lemon and Early Wynn each won twenty-three games. Mike Garcia posted a 19–8 record, and Bob Feller, at the ripe old age of thirty-five, compiled an excellent 13–3 mark.

The Indians were favored to defeat the New York Giants in the World Series, but it was not to be. Willie Mays and the rest of the Giants put on an incredible display of hitting and fielding, sweeping the Indians in four straight games. The 1954 season was the final moment of glory for several Cleveland stars, including Bob Feller, who finally retired after the 1956 season.

1 9 5 1

After a disappointing finish the previous year, Al Lopez was named the new Cleveland manager.

SUDDEN SAM STRIKES FEAR INTO HITTERS

Veteran righthander Dick Donovan paced Cleveland starters with 20 wins and a 3.59 ERA.

When Feller retired, Cleveland fans wondered if they would ever again see a pitcher who threw as hard as he did. It seemed unlikely that another Bob Feller would come along, but there was nothing likely about Sam McDowell, a left-handed pitcher who was called "the next Bob Feller" when he joined the Indians as an eighteen-year-old rookie in 1961. While growing up, McDowell never expected he would be good enough to become a major-leaguer. "I never really wanted to be a baseball player like the rest of the kids," McDowell recalled. "I just as easily could have been a teacher or had some other nine-to-five job. . . . But my father saw I had talent, so he forced me into it. But I never thought I was that good at it. Even when I made the majors, I never thought I was that good. I used to start every game with the hope I just wouldn't embarrass myself out there."

McDowell didn't have to worry about that. His fastball became one of the most feared in the major leagues. He soon acquired the nickname "Sudden" Sam because, as one player claimed, McDowell's pitches got to the plate "all of a sudden, man, all of a sudden." Some experts called McDowell the most talented pitcher in the majors. Said Oakland A's pitcher John "Blue Moon" Odom, "If I had Sudden's stuff, I'd win twenty-five games every year."

But McDowell wasn't really interested in winning twenty-five games every year; he was more concerned with overcoming challenges—personal challenges. "The only thing I get satisfaction from is accomplishing something I'm not supposed to be able to do," he stated. "I live for challenges, and once I overcome them, I have

Like McDowell, knuckleballer Tom Candiotti was a winner.

*Sam McDowell
(right) established a
team record for
lefthanders by
striking out 325
batters.*

to go on to something new. . . . A game to me is just a series of individual challenges—me against Reggie Jackson or me against Don Mincher. If I find I can get a guy out with a fastball, it takes all the challenge away, so next time I throw him all curveballs. If I don't have a challenge, I create one. It makes the game more interesting."

Most American League batters had little interest in trying to hit against McDowell. Oakland A's slugger Reggie Jackson, however, enjoyed the opportunity. "You know he's going to challenge you, his strength against yours, and either you beat him or he beats you," Jackson said. "And if you do beat him with a home run or something, it doesn't bother him that much. He's not greedy. He lets you have a little, too. And he won't throw at you, either, because he's too nice a guy. He knows that with his fastball, he could kill you if he ever hit you."

Another Indian lefty, Bud Black. 17

A Cleveland slugger from the early '80s, Joe Carter

The high kicking Gaylord Perry (right) joined the Indians in a trade with San Francisco.

Unfortunately for McDowell and the Cleveland fans, the Indians didn't enjoy much success during the 1960s. McDowell was named to the American League All-Star team six times, but he never came close to leading his team to a pennant. Cleveland didn't have many stars besides McDowell and power-hitting outfielder Rocky Colavito, who lad the American League in homers (forty-two) in 1959 and runs batted in (108) in 1965. The Indians roster was bolstered in 1971 by the addition of first baseman Chris Chambliss, who hit .275, drove in forty-eight runs, and was named Rookie of the Year in the American League.

McDowell's last year in Cleveland was 1971. He was traded in the off-season to the San Francisco Giants for veteran pitcher Gaylord Perry. When McDowell left Cleveland, he was second on the Indians' all-time strikeout list with 2,281. McDowell's total put him only three hundred strikeouts behind the legendary Bob Feller, and Feller had pitched seven more seasons for the Indians than McDowell had. Oddly, after leaving the Indians, McDowell never regained the form that had made him one of the top pitchers in baseball. Gaylord Perry, however, came to Cleveland in top form, and he would baffle American League hitters even more than McDowell had.

Oscar Gamble became the Indians' leading "designated hitter" with the introduction of the AL's new rule.

PERRY'S PITCHES PRODUCE SUCCESS

When Gaylord Perry joined the Indians he made it clear that he wouldn't settle for second best. Perry's philosophy was "You should do everything possible to win short of scratching the other guy's eyes out." Opponents believed Perry cheated to win by throwing spitballs, which are illegal. They accused Perry of putting Vaseline or grease or some other substance on the ball when he pitched. Even some of his teammates claimed Perry threw spitballs.

"There were games he might not throw many spitballs at all," recalled Kansas City catcher Fran Healy, who played with Perry in Cleveland. "It's the old psychological advantage—the hitters just thinking he's going to throw it. Nobody uses the spitter like that as well as Gaylord. He'll have you looking for it all day and get you out with other stuff." Perry himself said he didn't throw a spitball, but rather a forkball, a pitch that drops suddenly as it nears the plate. When Perry threw one of his "forkballs" that dropped a great deal, the opposing team would claim it was a spitball and ask the umpire to search Perry for grease or some other substance.

A fastball, shown here, was not Perry's best pitch.

Sometimes Perry practically had to undress on the mound so the umpire could search him, which angered his manager, Ken Aspromonte. "It's just that Gaylord is always the goat," the Cleveland manager said. "He has the reputation, so they [umpires] pick on him. Why don't they spread these searches around? Why just my guy? There are at least twenty other pitchers who should be examined." During his years in Cleveland, Perry was searched countless times, but the umpires never found what the opposing teams thought Perry was putting on the ball.

Andre Thornton tallied 116 RBI, the highest total in almost three decades of Cleveland baseball.

Perry's pitches, spitters or not, were almost unhittable in 1972. He won an amazing twenty-four games for a team that was never in contention for the pennant. For his efforts Perry was selected as the American League's Cy Young Award winner; he is the only Cleveland pitcher ever to receive that honor, which was first given in 1956. But the Cleveland club, even with Perry's heroics, remained near the bottom of the seven-team American League East Division throughout the 1970s and into the 1980s.

In an effort to reverse this trend Perry was traded after a few successful seasons, so Cleveland fans had to root for other stars, such as outfielder Joe Charboneau, who won the 1980 Rookie of the Year honor in the American League after batting .289, slugging twenty-three homers, and driving in eighty-seven runs. But Charboneau's star fell as quickly as it rose; he went into a long slump during the 1981 season and was sent down to the minor leagues. First baseman Andre Thornton picked up the slack by hitting thirty-two homers in 1982 and thirty-three more in 1984. In 1985, despite the presence of power

Left to right: Julio Franco, Greg Swindell, Chris James, John Farrell.

hitters such as Thornton, Joe Carter, and Mel Hall, the Indians lost 102 games, which tied the record for the most losses in franchise history. Cleveland rallied to post a winning season in 1986, and fans started to flock to Municipal Stadium to see such stars as Carter, center fielder Cory Snyder, and pitchers Tom Candiotti and Gregg Swindell. The Indians, however, were unable to build on this success and failed to become a championship-caliber team.

1 9 8 4

Second baseman Julio Franco set an Indian all-time record with 658 at-bats during the season.

The Cleveland club did manage to unleash at least one hidden talent during the late 1980s: Doug Jones rose from obscurity to become one of the top relief pitchers in the American League. Jones, who actually had to beg the Indians to give him a tryout, began baffling opposing hitters during the 1988 season. He did it with a devastating change-up, a pitch that traveled only about sixty miles an hour.

Earlier in his career, Jones tried to throw six different pitches. None of them really worked well, so he decided to concentrate on the fastball and the change-up. "The hardest part is accepting that you only have two pitches," Jones said. But those two pitches worked wonders. He totaled sixty-nine saves in 1988 and 1989 combined. Only Oakland standout Dennis Eckersley had more among American League pitchers.

Jones, however, wasn't overly impressed with his abilities. "When you go to an opera, you anticipate the tenor at the end," he said. "Instead, I'm like some guy who knows the words but can't sing. He just climbs up on stage and finishes the show. . . . There are no frills to my style. I just go out and take care of business."

The dependable Brook Jacoby (pages 26–27).

The Indians, though, weren't taking very good care of their business. After a disappointing 1989 season, in which the team finished sixth in the AL East with a 73–89 record, Cleveland officials decided to make a bold move. Joe Carter, one of the most feared sluggers in the American League, was traded to the San Diego Padres in a multi-player deal that included young catcher Sandy Alomar, Jr.

Doc Edwards led the Indians to within 11 games of the division title, their closest finish since 1959.

ALOMAR PROVES TO BE A BIG CATCH

The Indians were sorry to lose Carter, but team officials were easily consoled after seeing Alomar's talents. "I've been in baseball for twenty-nine years," said Cleveland bullpen coach Luis Isaac, "and Sandy Alomar is the best catching prospect I've seen since Johnny Bench." Alomar, who was born in Puerto Rico, certainly is one of the biggest catching prospects—he stands six feet five and weighs two hundred pounds. "You wait and see how much he develops as a hitter," Isaac said before the 1990 season. "He's only twenty-three years old now. He still has some baby fat. Most Latin players don't mature until they're twenty-six or twenty-seven."

Many Cleveland fans were worried that Alomar wouldn't want to leave San Diego, where his father, Sandy Alomar, Sr., was a coach. The catcher's brother, Roberto, was also with the Padres. "I had two feelings when the trade was made," said Alomar, who had been unable to beat out San Diego's All-Star catcher Benito Santiago for the starting position. "The first was that I was happy because I finally would have my chance. The second was that it was sad that the family was being

The talents of Cory Snyder (left) were an inspiration to young Sandy Alomar, Jr.

broken up. But we never had been together much anyway. I was in Las Vegas [playing for San Diego's top minor-league team]. My father and brother were in San Diego. What are you breaking up if you're only together in September anyway?"

If Alomar was homesick during his first season as an Indian, he showed no signs of it. His average hovered near .300 for much of the year, as the surprising Cleveland club fought its way into the middle of the AL East race. Alomar was so impressive that he was voted by the fans to start at catcher for the American League in the All-Star Game, making him only the third Cleveland player ever chosen as a starter for that team.

Although neither Alomar nor the Indians were able to sustain their torrid pace throughout the second half of the season, there were many signs indicating a promising

The talented Sandy Alomar, Jr.

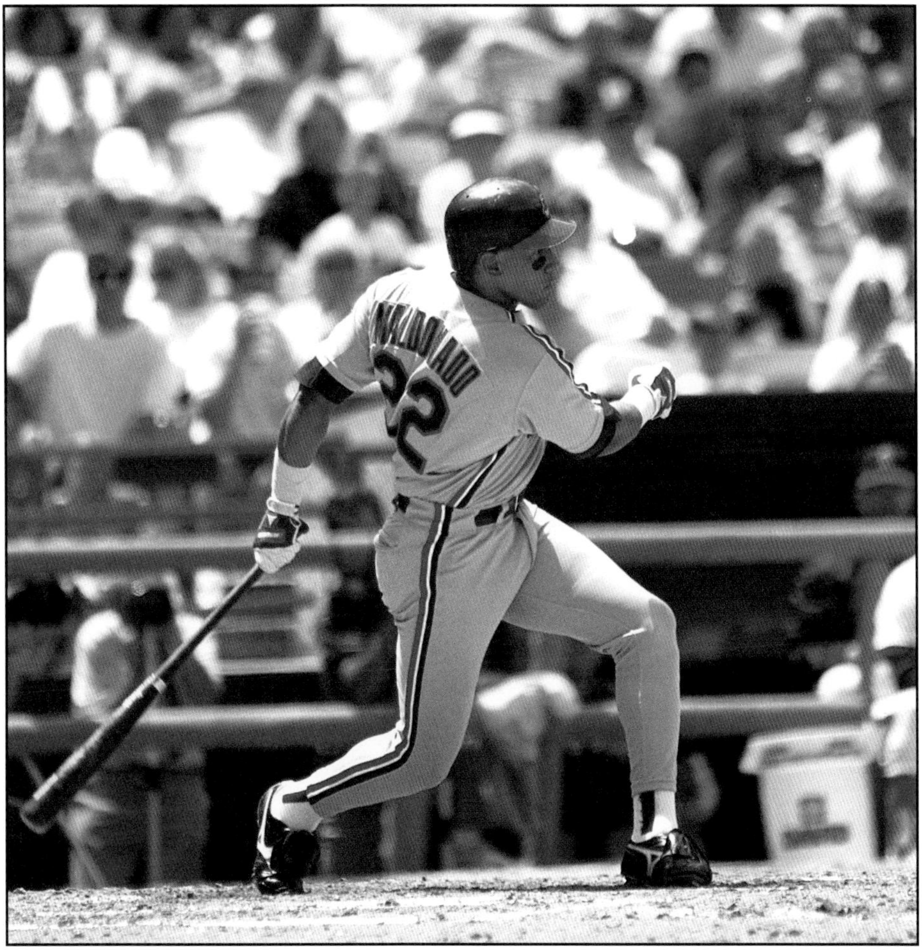

Candy Maldanado spent one season in Cleveland.

future. Infielder Brook Jacoby and outfielders Candy Maldonado, Cory Snyder, and Chris James keyed the Cleveland offense. Starting pitchers Tom Candiotti and Bud Black both had excellent years. Additionally, Doug Jones continued to show he was one of the top relief pitchers in the American League.

Thanks to these players, the Indians are hopeful of becoming a consistent contender in the American League East during the 1990s. Manager John McNamara, who led the Boston Red Sox to the 1986 World Series, knows what it takes to build a championship team, something the citizens of Cleveland would love to have.

DUE DATE